Buzz and Jack

Written by Jeanne Willis

Illustrated by Jennifer Davison

Collins

Buzz the chick is chums with Jack.

Jack the duck has a dip.

peck

Buzz tips off the bank.

Buzz sinks.

Jack gets him up.

Buzz has wet wings.

After reading

Letters and Sounds: Phase 3

Word count: 40

Focus phonemes: /j/ /w/ /zz/ /qu/ /ch/ /th/ /ng/ /nk/ /sh/

Common exception words: are, and, push, the, me

Curriculum links: Personal, Social and Emotional Development

Early learning goals: Reading: read and understand simple sentences; use phonic knowledge to decode regular words and read them aloud accurately; read some common irregular words

Developing fluency

- Your child may enjoy hearing you read the book.
- Ask your child to read the speech bubbles and sounds with expression, using a different tone for Buzz and Jack.

Phonic practice

- Read page 6. Ask your child to point to the two letters that make one sound in the words. (B/u/**zz**, o/**ff**, **th**/e, b/a/**nk**)
- Ask your child to sound out and blend the following words: s/i/nk/s, r/u/sh, qu/i/ck, w/i/ng/s, ch/u/m.
- Say the words and challenge your child to spell them out loud.
- Look at the "I spy sounds" pages (14–15). Take turns to find words in the picture containing a /j/ or /th/ sound. (e.g. *Jack, jelly, juice, jam (in the window), jump, thistle, moth, path, feathers*)

Extending vocabulary

- Ask your child:
  - What word could be used instead of **chums** on page 2? (e.g. *friends, pals, buddies*)
  - What words or phrases have a similar meaning to these: **has a dip** (page 4), **tips** (page 6), **rush** (page 9), **gets him up** (page 10)?
  - Discuss what the bank of a pond is like. Can you think of another meaning of **bank**? (e.g. *a place where money is kept*)